THINK
BIG!

To Mr & Mrs Elliott & Gemma Gray
K.G.
For Sam x
N.R.

HODDER CHILDRENS BOOKS

First published in Great Britain in 2019 by Hodder and Stoughton

Text copyright © Kes Gray, 2019
Illustration copyright © Nathan Reed, 2019

The moral rights of the author and illustrator have been asserted.

A CIP catalogue record for this book is available from the British Library.

HB ISBN: 978 1 444 94212 5

PB ISBN: 978 1 444 94213 2

10 9 8 7 6 5 4 3 2 1

Printed and bound in China

Hodder Children's Books, an imprint of Hachette Children's Group,
part of Hodder and Stoughton
Carmelite House, 50 Victoria Embankment, London, EC4Y 0DZ

An Hachette UK Company
www.hachette.co.uk

www.hachettechildrens.co.uk

MIX
Paper from
responsible sources
FSC® C104740

THINK BIG!

Written by
Kes Gray

Hodder Children's Books

Illustrated by
Nathan Reed

Humpty Dumpty was sitting on a wall
thinking about the future with his friends.

"What do you want to be
when you leave school?"
asked Tom Tom the Piper's Son.

"A BOILED EGG," said Humpty.

"A BOILED EGG!"

gasped the Three Blind Mice.

"YOU DON'T WANT TO
BE A BOILED EGG!"

"I'd make a very good boiled egg," said Humpty.

"You'd make a very **BIG** boiled egg,"

said Jack Be Nimble,
"but you still don't want
to be a boiled egg!"

"Get some scissors and become a hairdresser," said Baa Baa Black Sheep.

"Buy a pair of football boots and become a footballer," said Wee Willie Winkie.

"Learn to play
the guitar and
be a musician,"
said Mary Mary Quite Contrary.

"Look for clues and
become a detective,"
said Little Bo Peep.

"I want to be a scientist when I leave school," said Little Miss Muffet.

"Not a boiled egg?"

frowned Humpty.

"Definitely not a boiled egg," said Incey Wincey Spider.

"Honestly Humpty," said Jack and Jill,

"You might be an egg
but you really should try
thinking outside of the box."

"You could be
an artist!"

said Little Boy Blue.

"You could be a policeman!"

said Old King Cole.

"You could be a doctor!"

said Little Jack Horner.

"You could be
a firefighter!"
said Georgie Porgie.

"If you truly believe in yourself, and you work **really** hard,

then you can be
absolutely anything
in the world that
you want to be!"

said the Dish who ran
away with the Spoon.

"THINK BIG!"
said the Giant who lived at
the top of the beanstalk.

"Aim for the stars!"

said the Cow who jumped over the moon.

"YOU'RE RIGHT!"
said Humpty.

"When I grow up, I'm not going to be a boiled egg!

I'm going to work hard at school,

get a job in a space agency,

start at the bottom, work my way up and up and up and up and up and UP ...

... and become the best astronaut in the whole wide world,

no, the whole wide

UNIVERSE!"

"GOOD FOR YOU!" cheered Jack Be Nimble,
giving Humpty a BIG pat on the back ...

"On second thoughts,
make that an omelette,"
said Humpty.